Printed in the United States of America.

For more information, or to book an event, contact :
Email: kcl3rc@yahoo.com
www.lastdoorwayproductions.com

Editors : Reyna Young, Nicholas Grabowsky
Cover Image: Jason Dube
Colors Andy Tiu
Cover design by Reyna and John Gillette

ISBN – Paperback: 9798326196491

Second Edition:
10 9 8 7 6 5 4 3 2

THE WEREWOLF OF WOLF LAKE

Reyna Young

Last Doorway Press

For Logan, Zoey and Ezralynn

When you hear its howl

Under the full moon

You know it's near

And may meet your doom

1

Jimmy sprung up from bed, excited to start his birthday weekend off. He ran downstairs to see his parents eating breakfast. "Let's go!" he yelled out. His father smiled, knowing Jimmy had been excited for months about going to Wolf Lake for the week. Jimmy rushed his bags to the front door and quickly dressed. Grabbing a banana, he was ready to go.

His mom and dad packed the car and made sure lunches were made. Since it was a little more than a six-hour drive, they were going to need food for sure.

They hopped in the car and away they went. Jimmy, looking through the window as his father drove, couldn't hide his excitement over the thoughts of seeing his friends, having a great start to his birthday, and being able to sit by the fire at night and tell scary stories. As hours passed, Jimmy couldn't help but ask multiple times if they were there yet.

His father smiled, "We've been going here mostly every summer, except for last year, but you always ask the same thing every time we're driving...how long? Are we there yet? You're so funny."

Jimmy laughed, "Yeah, I know."

Jimmy's dad loved Wolf Lake. He'd been going there since he was a kid and his dad when he was a kid...it was kind of a family tradition, but what made it even more exciting was meeting up with his two best friends who went there every summer also: he couldn't wait to see Toby and Candice...

...especially because this year he had the scariest story to tell them around the campfire. This time he would scare Candice, who doesn't scare easily.

The sign flew passed.

Wolf Lake
20 miles to go

"Yay!" Jimmy yelled out, waiting to see that one last sign that they were there. He sat in the back eating his peanut butter sandwich – no jelly, he couldn't stand jelly. Once finished, the sign came zooming up.

Welcome to Wolf Lake

Jimmy smiled big, "We're here!" he yelled out, ready to kick off his birthday weekend. He was excited about this because he'd never gotten to spend his birthday at Wolf Lake before. Sure, it'd been fun every time he'd been up there...but for his birthday, it was extra special to him.

His father and mother glanced at each other over the smile on his face. They loved him so much.

"Are you ready, Jimmy?'

"I am," he excitedly yelled out.

His mom laughed, "You are too cute!"

Jimmy took a deep breath and looked down at one of his notebooks of scary stories he wrote, excited to tell them to his friends.

2

Jimmy's dad opened the door to their cabin and Jimmy ran in, "Cool."

Opening the door to his room and setting his bags down, he looked through the window to see Toby and Candice walking toward his cabin and jumped for joy as he ran out to see them. They both waved as they ran over.

"You're here!" Candice yelled out.

They all hugged each other, having a reunion they'd been waiting for since Jimmy skipped going last year due to his mom's new job not letting her have the time off.

Toby wiped the sweat off his forehead under his hat. "It's too hot out here for me and I think this is the hottest it's been."

Jimmy nodded, "It has to be."

"So, guess what tomorrow is?" Candice asked.

They both shrugged, "What?"

"Full moon," she smiled.

"Oh – cool, we'll be telling stories under the full moon, how cool!" Jimmy excitedly said.

"Speaking of stories, are you ready for tonight?" Toby grinned.

Jimmy laughed, "Of course I am."

"I hope you boys can scare me this time." Candice folded her arms.

"I've been writing a lot...trust me, you'll be scared from my story." Jimmy nodded.

"Sweet, I can't wait."

From afar Jimmy's mom yelled out for him to come back and finish up unpacking first before anything else.

Jimmy put his head down, "Ah man."

"It's fine, I have to finish unpacking too but I'll see you both tonight and I'll bring some cookies," Candice said before running back to her cabin.

Toby smiled, "I'm done unpacking so I can help you, if you like?"

"Sounds good to me."

They both went back to Jimmy's cabin and Toby helped him unpack his things. "What's with the backpack filled with notebooks?" he asked Jimmy.

"Oh – those are my notebooks of stories I've been working on."

"Whoa! That's a lot of writing."

"Told you, I've been practicing my art of

storytelling."

"Yeah, you have."

"I have so many stories I don't think I'll run out at all this trip."

Toby sat down on his bed, "I only wrote like three or four."

"Well, that's okay, I'm sure they're scary."

"Geez, I hope so."

"You tell good stories, so I don't doubt it."

"Thanks."

"You think Candice has something big up her sleeve?" Jimmy asked him.

Toby nodded, "Yeah."

"Ugh – I knew you were going to say that she always has the best stories."

"I know...she's hard to beat."

"Well, we'll see this time." Jimmy said with confidence. He was ready to scare her tonight, at least he hoped.

They looked over as someone knocked on his door, "Grandpa?" he smiled.

3

Jimmy's grandpa held out his arms, "Happy Birthday kiddo."

He ran up and hugged him...he hadn't seen him for a while. "What are you doing here?"

"I thought I'd surprise you and you know me; I love this place."

"I'm so glad you're here."

"Me too kiddo!" He waved at Toby, "Hi there, you got bigger?"

"I did, like four inches."

"Wow!"

"So, Grandpa, where are you staying?"

"I have a cabin over on the other side, more near the lake so I can go fishing in the mornings."

"Awesome."

"So, when are we doing the birthday cake?"

He laughed, "Tomorrow."

"Tomorrow? Ah- I want some now."

They both laughed, "Me too."

Jimmy's dad interrupted, "Hey pops, come check something out."

"Sure thing, I'll see you soon."

"Alright." Jimmy smiled.

Toby smiled, "That's cool your grandpa's here."

"Yeah, I had no idea he was going to be."

Jimmy's mom walked in, "Toby you are staying for dinner?"

"Sure!" he smiled.

"Great, it's spaghetti night."

"Cool." Toby nodded.

Jimmy looked over at Toby, "First dinner, then story time."

4

Toby, Candice, and Jimmy sat around the campfire staring at each other. They were each ready to tell their story, and Toby decided to go first.

"Alright, here's my story for night one… Once there was a woman who was too scared to leave the house, to have people see her, to even look at her own reflection. She made sure all the mirrors in her house were removed, all but one that stayed hidden in the attic, just in case she ever needed to look at herself. One night a burglar broke open the back door and walked in...he heard around town she was rich and wanted to steal as much money as he could from her. He walked upstairs and searched around the rooms for whatever he could find.

She was already awake when he began rummaging through the second room. She didn't know what to do; she quietly opened her door and walked out into the hall.

The burglar walked out at the right time to see her standing there. He looked right into her eyes and screamed as he turned to the stone. Little did he know he would be entering into Medusa's house."

Toby smiled at his scary story. "That was pretty good right?" he asked them.

They both nodded yeah, and Candice laughed a bit because she didn't think it was so scary. Jimmy jumped to be next, raising his hand in the air, "My turn."

"Alright." Candice said, waiting for him to read.

Jimmy took a deep breath and opened his notebook...

"One dark and stormy night, there was a girl named Shelley who was invited to a sleepover. She wasn't just any girl but the most popular girl in school, so being invited was a big deal to Shelley. Once Shelley arrived at Joan's house, she saw some of the other girls there as well who were a part of Joan's click.

As they went on through the night eating ice cream and talking about boys, Shelley came up with an idea to play a game. At first Joan and her friends didn't want to play anything, thinking games were for little kids, but eventually Shelley convinced them it would be fun. Now Shelley began to tell them the rules of the game: once in front of the mirror you cannot look away, you must continue staring even after you say Bloody Mary three times. Joan wanted to go first, so she stood in front of her bathroom mirror, in the dark, while the others stood outside waiting for something to happen.

Joan looked intently at her bathroom mirror and began to say the words Bloody Mary, Bloody Mary, Bloody Mary. Once finished she continued looking into the mirror to see something, then she opened her mouth to scream but nothing would come out. After a few minutes, Shelley and the other girls opened the bathroom door to find Shelley wasn't there. To this day no one knows exactly what happened that night, only that Joan is still missing to this day."

Toby leaned back, "Whoa! That was scary."

Candice clapped, "Not bad Jimmy, not bad

at all."

Jimmy looked over at her, "Your turn."

Candice smiled...

"One dark and stormy night, a girl was wandering through the woods and had no idea how she got there. The only thing she remembered was sleeping in her bed. If she was safe and sound in her bed, then why was she in the woods suddenly? Her feet covered in mud, she walked and walked, trying to figure out how to get out of there...she wasn't sure which way was north or south. She was scared, cold and wanting to go home.

She walked for what seemed like forever until she spotted a small cottage with smoke coming out of its chimney. She ran over, pounding on the door. But no one answered. She pounded once more, and the door opened on its own. She slowly stepped inside, looking around for signs of anyone, but the place was empty. As she drew closer to the noise coming from the tiny living room, the lights came on and a cup of tea was sitting on a tiny table. She was going to grab it, being so thirsty from hours of walking, but then came a noise from upstairs.

She slowly walked up the stairway, hoping someone was on the second floor to help her. She pushed open a door to find no one there, and she gazed around until she noticed a closet door, which looked familiar. She walked over, placed her hand upon the knob and opened it. What she saw was her bedroom from her house, and memories came flooding back. She tried to walk through the closet, back to her bedroom, but couldn't. Then a strange growling noise came from behind her. She turned around and then screamed, for what she saw was the Boogeyman and he had her trapped."

"Whoa!" Todd said.

Jimmy nodded, "That was good."

She smiled, "I know."

Jimmy's grandfather walked up and sat down, "What you kids doing?"

"Telling scary stories." She said.

He smiled, "How fun, can I tell one."

"Yeah." They all screamed in excitement.

"It's pretty scary though."

"Bring it," they all said.

5

He began, "Many many moons ago, a family used to vacation here every summer. Now this family was no ordinary family, but a family of wolves. You see, this was the only place where they felt safe enough to transform and run around freely in the woods. Now this family grew, their kids had kids who were wolves and so on and every year they found themselves coming back to not only be freely safe but to also let the little ones know who they were and where they came from.

Now – one year a body was found in the woods; the horrible act had rumors flying all around town and the camp site here that it was the work of werewolves, but it was not true. A werewolf who was out one night witnessed what had happened but could not come forward due to not being able to explain why they were out so late in the woods. This burdened him and his family; it took those years before they could come back again to feel it was okay to roam around at night. They had left just in the nick of time too, as the locals gathered to hunt down these wolves and kill them all.

Now that it's been so long and the family now returned, it was time for a new generation to find out who they were, so you better be careful roaming about out here at night, you may see one yourself."

They all sat there in shock. Candice looked

over at everyone, "Whoa!"

Jimmy's grandpa sat up, "Good night kids," and walked back to his cabin.

"There are wolves out here?" Toby asked.

"Nah..." Jimmy reluctantly said. "Maybe."

Candice laughed, "Didn't you hear him, guys? There are wolves in these woods."

Toby chuckled, "Say that ten times."

Candice laughed, "Let's go, let's go wolf hunting tomorrow night when the moon is full?"

Toby and Jimmy looked at each other. "I don't know, it kind of sounds like a bad idea if you ask me," he said.

Jimmy thought for a moment. He didn't seem scared by the idea...in fact it intrigued him, "I'm down."

"Yeah!" Candice jumped for joy.

Toby didn't want to feel left out so he

agreed. Tomorrow night they would go werewolf hunting and see if they could spot one. The moon was nearly full, so it should be a good night for them to go. They all went off to their cabins to get some rest and plan tomorrow out after breakfast.

Jimmy couldn't wait.

6

Jimmy was so excited to go werewolf hunting that he could hardly sleep. He tossed and turned and no matter what he did, he just could not sleep. He sat up in bed taking in a deep breath, and that was when he heard it: a loud howling coming from outside. He quickly ran over to his window and looked out at the side of the curtain. Standing there with glowing yellow eyes was a werewolf.

His jaw dropped. "What?" he whispered. It was glaring at him as he glared back, and he couldn't believe his eyes. Was he dreaming or was this for real? He snuck out of his bedroom and stepped quietly to the front door. Opening it, he walked outside to see that it was gone. He looked around but it was nowhere to be seen, then just as he was closing the door a howl came from within the nearby woods, and he shut and locked the door immediately. He couldn't wait to tell the others.

The next day, Jimmy ran over after breakfast to Candice's to meet up with her and Toby.

Candice smiled, "Ready for game plan meeting?"

Jimmy frowned, "Meeting?"

"Yeah," she maintained her grin.

"Can we at least go outside and plan it? It's so nice out."

Candice laughed, "Of course, silly." She

grabbed her notebook and away they went.

"Jimmy began to tell them about his weird night and that he saw the werewolf, and Toby and Candice both declared that they heard it as well. Candice thought it was weird that his grandfather told them that story and then all of a sudden, they heard it and Jimmy saw it.

She began to write down her game plan. "First we wait until our parents are asleep, then we all sneak out and meet up at the campfire section where we can start walking into the woods there since there's a path."

"Whoa!" How late are we talking?" asked Toby.

"Well, I guess midnight."

"I guess that's okay, I want to get a nap in before we go."

Jimmy laughed, "Of course you do."

Candice continued, "Then we bring

backpacks full of waters, flashlights and whatever else you think we need."

"Like weapons," Toby said, getting a candy bar out of his pocket.

"Sure," Candice said, "but we don't want to hurt it."

"But what if it attacks us?" Jimmy asked. "It is a werewolf."

"Then we run I guess," she answered.

"Sounds fair to me," Toby said.

Jimmy nodded, "All right."

Candice tried to think of anything else that they should bring but nothing came to mind. She figured they were pretty much ready to go, but until then they walked over to the lake to enjoy the ducks. Jimmy saw his grandfather and father there fishing off to the side, and he waved to them. Toby and Candice waved too.

"We should ask your grandfather more

about the werewolves," she said.

Jimmy shrugged, "I don't know, maybe later, they look like they're talking about something."

"Okay. How about at your birthday dinner tonight?" asked Toby.

"Sure," he said.

7

They all sat around the dinner table for spaghetti – Jimmy's favorite. Toby was especially excited since he loved Jimmy's mom's cooking. They all served themselves some salad and spaghetti.

Candice took a bite, "Yummy."

Grandfather smiled over at her.

"I have a question for you."

He smiled again, "Sure?"

"Is there anything else you can tell us about the werewolves that roam around here?"

Jimmy's dad practically choked on his pasta, and they all stopped to stare at him.

"You are still telling that tale, Dad?" he asked him.

"Of course...it's true."

"Ha — so it is true," Candice dramatically said.

Toby and Jimmy looked at her and she shrugged her shoulders. "Sorry."

Jimmy laughed, "Yeah...Grandpa, is there anything else we need to do about the werewolves? Because last night I didn't just hear one, I saw one."

His grandfather sat there thinking for a moment. "Are you sure you saw it?"

"Oh yes, with my own two eyes."

"Looks like if you saw one, then you should all know that they're real."

"We do," Toby said.

Jimmy's dad laughed. "Are you sure you didn't all have the same dream? Seeing how my pops here told you a werewolf story, you all had werewolf on the brain. It may have just been a dream."

"It wasn't though, Dad! I saw it, I went outside and looked for it after it left, but it was gone."

Jimmy's mom's jaw dropped. "You went outside...when?"

Jimmy frowned, "Last night."

His grandfather began laughing. "You went out chasing a werewolf! You are one brave kid."

"Are they really dangerous?" he asked.

Jimmy's dad said yes, and his grandfather said no at the same time. They both looked at each other and shook their heads at one another.

"Dad, don't tell them that."

"Why not, it's true; they're friendly, not dangerous at all."

Candice smiled, "That's good to know."

Toby nodded his head, "Yeah, I guess."

Jimmy was confused, "I thought werewolves were dangerous though, they attack and kill people?"

"Not all of them, some are nice," his grandfather explained.

His dad chimed in, "But you always want to be aware, because they can be dangerous."

Jimmy thought, "Yeah, like anything or anyone."

His dad smiled, "Exactly."

They all finished off their dinner and then the birthday cake. They sang and ate, and after headed to Jimmy's room to plan for the night.

Jimmy shut the door behind him, "Okay, I am so ready for tonight; let's go hunt us a wolf."

"As long as we're careful," Toby said.

"Of course," Candice rolled her eyes.

Jimmy showed them his only flashlight but thought he could get more from his dad's things…there was no need, Candice, and Toby both had their own from their parents.

"So tonight," Candice whispered, "remember, we'll meet in the middle of the campfire area and go from there, at midnight."

His mom knocked on his door with a plate of cookies and three glasses of milk.

They all thanked her. Toby took a bite of his warm chocolate chip cookie, "Your mom is the best."

Jimmy smiled, "I know, I told her cake was enough."

Toby smiled, "No. it's not."

They sat there eating and gathering things from around the room for Jimmy's backpack, like a few waters and any weapons they thought they should bring, Toby mentioned he was going to bring his baseball bat just in case, so they agreed that was enough. They parted ways and prepared for midnight separately.

8

As soon as Jimmy quietly shut the door, he ran over to the campfire area, meeting with Toby and Candice. They were there, waiting for him.

"What do we do now?" Toby whispered to Candice.

"Now, we walk."

They turned on their flashlights and headed into the woods. Jimmy wasn't feeling too well, for some reason he developed a bad stomachache but didn't tell the others. He didn't want to dampen the mood of wolf hunt for them. They walked through the woods looking for any clues about a wolf or a wolf itself. They were determined to find one or more. Toby was the most nervous though, and his hand shook as he held his flashlight.

As they moved on further, Candice sighed over the fact that there were no clues, let alone no wolf.

"How long are we going to be out here?" Toby asked.

"Keep it down, we should whisper when we're out here," she said.

Toby agreed, whispering to her, "Okay, how long are we going to be out here?"

Candice smiled, "I don't know, until we're tired."

Jimmy chuckled, "I knew you'd say that."

Candice stopped, and they all stopped. "Did you hear that?"

"No," Toby whispered.

Candice flashed her light around. "I swear I heard something."

They continued walking when she heard a cackling noise coming from within the trees. "Did you hear that?"

"Yeah," they both answered.

They journeyed a little bit further when they heard a howling not far away from them. They all stopped in their tracks and exchanged glances.

"The wolf," Jimmy whispered.

Then the tree branches around them began to move, and Jimmy flashed his light around the bushes and trees. He flashed by to see something staring at him "Oh no," he exclaimed under his breath.

Toby and Candice looked over, "Wolf."

The werewolf stepped out from the trees, glaring at them.

"Run!" Toby yelled out.

They all ran out of the woods and back to their cabins. Jimmy turned around at his doorway once inside, and there again was the wolf just a little way away, still giving that same frightening glare.

He closed the door behind him and ran to his room, hastening to his window to see it sitting out there with its glowing eyes.

9

Toby and Candice met up with Jimmy at the lake where everyone was out enjoying the sun. They began to talk about what had happened the previous night.

Candice sat on the grass. "I knew it was real, your grandfather knows way more than he's leading on...you know that, right?"

Jimmy nodded, "Oh, I know." He kept on holding his stomach. "I don't feel too well," he said.

"What's wrong?" Toby asked.

"I don't know, ever since last night I started getting these stomach pains. My dad said they'd go away, but it keeps coming off and on."

"That's weird," Toby said.

"I know."

They continued talking until Jimmy looked over to see Tommy the bully heading their direction, "Oh no!"

Candice and Toby looked over to see Tommy as well. Toby rolled his eyes and Candice let out a sigh, "I thought this was going to be fun until I saw him."

Tommy walked up to them, "Well, look who we have here."

They all rolled their eyes.

"Don't you have somewhere else to be?" Jimmy asked.

Tommy laughed. "Little geeky Jimmy, I'm shocked you showed your face after what happened last year."

"Leave him alone, Tommy," Candice said.

Tommy, still laughing, couldn't help himself, "You know, I would love to see you try to swing from the rope again, maybe this time you'll fall in the water."

Candice, Toby, and Jimmy stood up; "It's time for you to leave" Toby said.

Jimmy stood there with his head down, trying not to let him get to him.

"What's wrong, Jimmy? You can't stick up for yourself?"

"I can too," he proclaimed, angry.

"Yeah, right," he said in his face.

Jimmy's blood began to boil; he was mad, so mad he lost his temper, something he never did. He rushed forward, pushing Tommy, pushing him so hard Tommy flew back in the air and into the lake.

They stood there in shock. Jimmy didn't know what to think of what he just did, and he ran off.

Toby and Candice continued laughing at Tommy attempting feebly to get out of the water.

10

That night, Jimmy couldn't sleep. He tossed and turned once again. Since he couldn't sleep, he looked out his window to see if the werewolf was there, and it wasn't. He went back into this bed, and it wasn't until hours later that he finally fell out.

When he awoke in the morning his sheets were covered with dirt and his feet up to his ankles were too, and he shook his head and gazed on…. he couldn't believe what he was seeing. What happened last night?

He met up with Candice and Toby's at Candice's cabin to let them know what he woke up to.

They both agreed that he was probably sleepwalking. Jimmy had never sleepwalked before, so he didn't think it was that at all. Candice on the other hand thought maybe it was more than that...she didn't know yet, but she was starting to think that maybe the werewolf was calling out to him, and she wanted to speak with his grandfather more, so they decided to head over to his cabin and have a chat with him.

When they arrived, his grandfather opened the door and gave him a great big hug. He let them in and got them all some water. "Must stay hydrated in this heat. Remember that, especially you, Jimmy."

"Me?"

"Yes, you have to drink lots of water."

He nodded, "All right." But thought it was weird he'd say that.

Candice drank some water. "Thank you, I was wondering if we can talk to you some more about werewolves?"

He chuckled, "Werewolves huh? I'm guessing you're all a bit obsessed over them now."

"Yes," they all said simultaneously.

He chuckled once again, "What is it that you would like to know?"

Candice thought for a moment. "Well...first off, how do you know about them?"

He leaned back in his chair. "Well...you see, I used to go here for the summers with my parents and I saw one."

"You did?" Toby asked, surprised.

"Yes, I did, and it was scary and fun all at the

same time. I saw one, one night after dinner. I went for a little walk, and it was there in the bushes, staring at me."

"What did you do?" Jimmy asked. "Well, I ran all the way back to my cabin and hid under my blankets, it scared me so bad." He began laughing, "I've been coming back ever since, bringing your father and now he brings you."

"Wow!" Candice said, "That's so cool."

Jimmy drank some more water. "Why does Dad deny the whole werewolf thing?"

"He's never seen one, so of course I can see him not believing."

"That makes sense," Candice responded. "How can we find out more about who this werewolf can be?"

"I'm not sure about that, I read lots of books and you should too."

"My dad has some folklore books with

werewolf stuff in them we can check out," Candice said.

"That's good, start there."

They all nodded their heads. Candice thanked him once again for the waters and off they went back to Candice's cabin to look at her dad's books.

11

Candice grabbed a few books down off a shelf in her dad's room to show them what she had found before...a few chapters on werewolves, but that wasn't enough for her; she wanted to learn more.

Toby and Jimmy scanned through the chapters. Candice continued talking about how she had a theory...she may know who the werewolf was. She kept saying how it had to be a family who kept coming back every year, that's why there are wolves. If the reason they can roam free and be okay is because they know this place and the woods inside and out, it must be someone they know or have met.

Jimmy agreed with her, saying that he thought the same thing, but now they had to narrow it down to who it could be.

Toby thought for a moment before telling them that they may have to investigate before narrowing down their suspects. Candice agreed and they headed out the door to have a look around. It was another beautiful day for folks to be out and about, so they looked around.

Toby pointed over toward the Henderson's who came out every year, but Jimmy argued that they couldn't be werewolves because the Henderson's were always out late in front of their cabin sitting down, watching the sky. During a full moon they wouldn't be seen.

Candice agreed and they continued; she

looked over at the Smiths who always went to sleep early and woke up extra early. Jimmy and Toby wrote them down as potential suspects.

As they continued, Jimmy began to feel stomach pains again...he didn't know what was wrong with him or why they kept coming back off and on.

He told them that as much as he wanted to continue, he had to go back to his cabin, he wasn't feeling good. Jimmy made his way back and jumped under the covers. He felt so cold, like he was getting chills. He was hoping it wasn't the flu. His mom covered him up and he remained in bed for the rest of the day and night.

12

Jimmy awoke in the morning feeling a lot better. He didn't know what was wrong with him, only that whatever it was, had passed. He swung off his blankets to find his legs and feet covered in dirt. He screamed, "What is this?"

His mom called out, asking if he was okay, and he yelled back out that he was fine and covered his legs back up before she opened his bedroom door.

"You sure?"

"Yeah, I feel great, actually."

"That's good, now wash up – breakfast is almost done."

"Okay Mom."

He jumped in the shower right away and then cleaned up his bed sheet as much as possible. After breakfast he met up with Candace and Toby to let them know what happened. They both thought it was weird; Candice couldn't quite put her nose on it, "Maybe you were sleepwalking?" she guessed.

Toby agreed, "Yes!"

"I've never slept walked before."

"That doesn't mean you can't start at any time. I mean think about it, lately we've been chasing a werewolf so it's natural for you to maybe sleepwalk a bit and look for it yourself since it's on the brain."

Toby sat there confused, "I see what you're saying but I don't know, maybe."

"Come on, you know I'm right."

"Maybe."

Candice laughed, "You have a better idea?"

He shook his head, "Nope."

"Well, then."

Jimmy couldn't make any sense from it, "I'm confused, why would I sleep-walk. It makes no sense."

"I have an idea," Candice yelled out. "What if we slept over tonight and watched you?"

Jimmy agreed, "That sounds great, I would love to have you over and watch out for me. I need to know what I do after I fall asleep."

Toby shrugged his shoulders, "I hope I can stay awake."

Candice laughed, "I'll make sure you do."

13

Candice and Toby made themselves comfortable on the floor in their sleeping bags. Jimmy was excited for them to stay over and help him out, hoping they would get to the bottom of what happened last night. Even though it wasn't the plan, they ended up staying up a little later than they wanted to.

Jimmy was the first to fall asleep, and right after that Toby began to fall out and then Candice. Hours passed and they were all snoring away.

A howling noise from outside awoke

Candice who quickly sat up, remembering she was supposed to stay awake. She looked over at Jimmy, who was not in his bed.

"Oh no." she whispered. Jumping out of her sleeping bag, she shook Toby, who did not want to wake up. She ditched Toby and walked out the bedroom door to find the front door open. She walked out into the cold to look for Jimmy, but she didn't know where to find him. She stayed there to see if he would come back but he didn't. Through the darkness she could hardly see anything, and then the sound of a wolf echoed through Wolf Lake, not just one but two howls.

Candice shook in fear. She shut the door behind her and ran back to Jimmy's room. She didn't know what to do or what to think...he was out there, and it was unsafe for him...if something bad were to happen, she'd blame herself.

She lay there in her sleeping bag with thoughts racing through her head a mile a minute and began to grow tired. Eventually she fell asleep, still wondering where Jimmy went.

The next morning, she awoke to find both Jimmy and Toby gone. She could faintly hear them in the kitchen, and she went over to see them making themselves some breakfast and laughing in the kitchen.

"Jimmy."

He looked up, "Morning."

She walked toward them. "What happened last night?"

He laughed, "We all fell asleep."

"What? No!"

Toby nodded his head, "Yeah, we did."

"I woke up in the middle of the night and you were gone, Jimmy."

"I was?"

"Yeah, I went outside looking and I couldn't find you anywhere and I heard a wolf- not one but two."

"What?"

Jimmy's mom walked into the kitchen. "What do we have here?"

"Making you breakfast, mom."

"Awe...well you're all up early this morning."

"Yup," Toby said.

"What's for breakfast?" she asked.

"Pancakes!" Jimmy excitedly yelled out.

"Great. I'm going to make some coffee for your father and I, he's still in bed."

Candice's eyes widened. She figured out who the werewolves were: they were Jimmy's parents. Now, how was she going to tell him his parents were werewolves?

14

Later in the day, Candice went off to do some research of her own by talking to her dad who knew a great deal about Wolf Lake. She sat with her glass of milk at the kitchen table and asked him, "How long have you been coming to Wolf Lake?"

"Well, since you turned six, we've been coming here."

"No, I meant before I was born, how long were you coming here before I was born?"

He thought for a moment. "Wow...um, well – I guess you can say since I was in my teens but it's not like we came out every summer or vacation or spring break or anything, there were years we didn't come out. Why you ask?"

"You know my friend Jimmy...you know his parents, right?"

"Well, yeah, we went to high school together."

"When you were coming out here, was his family out here too?"

"They came out here whenever they could, they love this place."

"I see." She nodded.

"Why? What's going on?"

"I can't tell you." She slouched down in her chair.

"Why not?"

"Because you'll think I'm weird."

He laughed, "I'm not going to think that at all, sweetheart."

She took a deep breath, "I think Jimmy's parents are werewolves."

He began laughing; she crossed her arms, giving him a dirty look.

"I knew I shouldn't have told you."

"No, no sweetie, I'm not laughing at you. I think maybe you're reading too many scary books lately."

"No, I'm not. I mean it, I'm going to investigate them more closely."

Her dad chalked it off to her having a big imagination, "You do that and tell me what you find out."

"Really?" Still crossing her arms.

"Yes, I mean it. Let me know what you find

out."

"Okay."

"You know what kiddo? If you really want to talk to someone about werewolves around here you should go see Maggie Hall, she's four cabins down from us. She's been coming here for ages."

She thought for a moment, "I may do that."

She walked four cabins down to see an older woman sitting on a rocking chair reading a book; they looked at each other and smiled. She was a bit nervous but asked her if she was Maggie. She nodded and invited her up.

"I was wondering if I can talk to you about something?" she asked nervously.

Maggie nodded, "Sure thing."

"Do you know anything about werewolves?"

"You mean the werewolves who have been

hanging around here for quite some time?"

Her jaw dropped, "Yeah."

"I know that they've been around for centuries and that the ones I have seen have glowing eyes."

"Are – are they dangerous?"

"I'm not sure, I've never heard of them causing any problems, only running around.

But I have heard many others say not to go near them just in case."

She nodded, "Okay."

"Have you seen one?"

"I – I kind of."

"Be careful girl," she interrupted. "You never know – they may turn you into one of them."

She got scared. "Th - thank you for your t - time," she stuttered before quickly leaving...the woman had her worried about turning into one.

The woman yelled out, "Don't let it scratch you."

She turned around and nervously smiled at her. "Thank you again."

She went off to the lake to spy on Jimmy's dad and grandfather who were sitting down fishing. She sat across and watched them, pretending to read a book.

Jimmy and Toby snuck up behind her. "Boo!" they yelled out.

She jumped up from the grass.

15

Jimmy laughed, "What are you up to?" She pushed him, "I wasn't scared."

Toby sat down, "Sure you weren't."

Jimmy sat down and looked around. Candice kept glancing over at Jimmy, picturing him as a werewolf.

Toby looked over, "Here we go again."

They looked over to see Tommy heading their way.

"Don't talk to him, Jimmy," Candice said.

"I'm not."

Tommy didn't stop to bully them this time. He walked on by, not even looking at them.

Toby and Candice exchanged glances with Jimmy. "Did you see that?"

Jimmy nodded, "Yeah that was kind of weird."

"Well, if you think about it, not really. I mean last time he saw you; you practically threw him across the world."

They all laughed, and Jimmy felt good about Tommy walking by and not bothering them. They sat there for a little longer, talking about going hunting again, but all Jimmy could think about was how good his hearing was suddenly. It sounded like he could hear his father and grandfather talking from afar. As he looked on at them, he could hear his grandfather talking about telling him something, but what?

As he stared at them, trying to figure out what they were talking about, his grandfather looked over at him, staring him right in the eyes. It was as if he knew he was listening to them.

Jimmy quickly looked away, pretending he wasn't spying on them.

Candice continued trying to get his attention; she waved her hand in front of his face, "Hello."

"I'm sorry."

"Where did you go?"

"I was just...daydreaming I guess."

"So, what do you think?"

"About what?" he asked.

"About us sleeping over again, we can watch another horror film and watch out for you again."

"Sounds good but first we should hit the

campfire and tell some more stories."

Toby smiled, "That sounds like a fun night to me."

"Perfect, cannot wait," Candice nodded, playing it cool. With only one more night of the full moon, she knew this was her night to catch him in the act of becoming a wolf.

16

Jimmy met up with Toby and Candice at the campfire to gather for story time. He sat down with his notebook. "I'm ready."

Toby shook his head, "I have nothing guys, it's you two."

"What? What do you mean you have nothing?"

"I can't think of anything, you guys are way better at telling stories then I am."

Candice shrugged her shoulders, "Alright, Jimmy – you want to go first?"

"How about you go first."

Candice smiled, "Okay."

"Take it away," Toby excitedly said.

Candice began...

"Once there was a little boy named Greg and Greg loved to watch the rain fall outside his bedroom window. Now one night, Greg was watching the rain when he saw something...someone standing there watching him. This creeped him out, and he immediately shut his curtains and went straight to bed. Minutes later he was awakened by the rain coming into his bedroom, and his window was open; he looked around his bedroom before getting up and closing it. After he closed it, he went back into bed and covered himself up from the cold that was let in. He thought nothing of his window being open, thinking maybe the wind had pushed it.

He fell back asleep but hours later he was awakened once again by his window open and the rain coming in. Tired and upset he had to get back up out of bed, he walked over to the window and shut it once again.

Before he made it to his bed his closet door creaked open. He stopped and looked over to see the door slowly opening. He jumped back into his bed and covered his head with his blanket. Lying there he could hear his door open a little bit more, then footsteps heading toward his bed. Whoever it was then stopped, and he knew it was staring at him, he could feel it.

Greg slowly lowered his blanket and with one eye peeked out to look around his room. He didn't see anyone around. He lowered the rest of his blanket and saw nothing, but his closet door was still open. He thought maybe he was just tired and seeing and hearing things. He shook it off, thinking it was nothing. But instead of going back to sleep he decided to get up and shut his closet door. Once his feet hit the ground two hands popped out from under his bed, grabbed his ankles and dragged him under. Never to be seen again."

Toby's jaw dropped down, "That was scary, Candice."

"Thank you." She smiled.

Jimmy shook his head, "Okay, that was good. Now it's my turn."

"Okay Jimmy, scare me." Candice said.

17

Jimmy began...

"A young woman was walking home late at night. The night was foggy, wet from the rain earlier and her car wouldn't start, that's why she walked. As she was enjoying her walk, a shadowy figure passed by her from up above. She looked up toward the sky, saw nothing. She continued walking. She was only blocks away from her house when the shadowy figure flew over her once again. She stopped, looking up to see what it could have been. A bird, an animal of some sort jumping from tree to tree, it could be anything, she thought. Instead of continuing to get home she stood there watching the sky, to see if maybe she could catch a glimpse of whatever it was.

She stood there for a few seconds waiting, and then something flew by again, something big, something she'd never seen before, and it looked like a giant moth. Scared out of her mind she began to run, run as fast as she could; she ran up the steps of her house, getting out her keys. She was so scared she dropped them, and the flying moth overhead swooped down and grabbed her, taking her away.

Her screams could be heard throughout the neighborhood until she was so far away no one could hear her. She was never seen again, and neither was the giant moth creature."

Toby, with his hand over his mouth, was speechless.

Candice smiled, "Not bad Jimmy, not bad at all."

Toby nodded, "Yes, I really liked them both, both stories were really good."

They thanked him and headed to Jimmy's to watch a film and sleep over again.

As they walked Candice asked him, "How have you been feeling today?" She was curious to know if he was still feeling sick or not.

"I've been feeling good today, the stomach pains stopped, the weird body aches. I'm feeling a lot better. It must have been a weird flu or something."

"Yeah, weird," she agreed and left it alone; she knew tonight was the night to figure this whole thing out...

Was her best friend a werewolf?

18

After the movie they were all feeling tired, so they went to bed. Candice's plan was to fake sleep so she could find out where he went when he sleepwalked. Toby was the first to fall, of course, and he always was.

An hour passed and she could hear Jimmy snoring a bit, and she thought this was it...all she had to do now was wait. She lay there in bed staring up at the ceiling. A few times his father opened the door to check up on them, that's when she closed her eyes and pretended to be sleeping. After the third time his father checked on them, she began to think how weird it was that he did...it seemed a little odd for him to check so many times.

As another hour passed. Candice did her best to stay awake. She was falling asleep off and on but made sure she took deep breaths and did her best to keep her eyes opened.

Toby's loud snoring helped keep her up; she was surprised that Jimmy was sleeping through it.

Jimmy sat up in bed, with his eyes still closed.

Candace noticed movement and sat up in her sleeping bag. This was it; it was happening.

Jimmy got out of bed and headed toward his bedroom door. Candace waited a few moments and then got up, and she tried to wake up Toby, but he wouldn't stir...he was snoring away.

She put on her shoes fast and headed out the bedroom door in a hurry. She saw Jimmy walking out the front door, and she ran over and out after him, pausing to close the door quietly so no one else would wake up. She followed him into the woods, making sure to stay a bit behind so she didn't get caught.

She stopped and looked around. She couldn't find him, and before she knew it, she could hear wolves howling. She stood there frozen, not knowing what to do, whether she should run back or not.

She looked around in the dark but couldn't see much, until a wolf stepped up to her. She stopped, looked it in the eyes and could tell it was Jimmy, it was his eyes. The wolf backed away from her, howling up toward the moon before running off.

Candice turned around and ran off, heading

back to the cabin, and she was scared. As she ran back, she stopped seeing another wolf run past her, and she almost screamed but contained herself. Continuing to run off, she opened the front door and ran in, back into Jimmy's room and under her sleeping bag. Her mind spinning a mile a minute and her heart beating fast, she didn't know what to think anymore.

She lay there staring back up at the ceiling thinking about what she saw until she fell asleep. With all the excitement you'd think she wouldn't even be able to fall asleep, but because she was so exhausted her body needed the rest.

The next morning, she awoke to Toby and Jimmy gone, and she walked out into the kitchen to see them there eating breakfast.

19

"How are you feeling Jimmy?" she asked him. He smiled and told her he was feeling great and that he slept like a baby.

Did he know, did he not know? She was beyond confused and didn't want to ask him in fear his parents would hear.

They all ate breakfast, and she did her best to play off that she knew anything. Toby and Jimmy ran outside, excited to go to the lake; she grabbed her things and followed after them.

Jimmy's father waved goodbye to them and gave Candice a weird look, or so she thought. She couldn't help but feel a little paranoid now. She continued walking with them and when they arrived at the lake, she thought now would be a good time to talk to Jimmy, but Jimmy spoke before she could… "You know, I was thinking maybe we shouldn't go chasing these werewolves, they might be dangerous you know, plus no more full moons."

Toby agreed. "That sounds like a great idea, I would hate to be food for them."

They laughed.

Candice was shocked he would say that after he was so excited to look for them also. "Well, the full moon is gone now so I guess it wouldn't make sense."

"Exactly my point, I think what we saw was a big dog and that's all," Jimmy said.

She could tell he was doing his best to guide them in a different direction; of course, Toby would agree and move on from it, he'd always been a scaredy cat. She agreed though, figured why not move on from it but keep an eye on him, whether he knew or he didn't.

Jimmy's grandfather came walking up. "Howdy kids."

They all said hello. Jimmy gave him a great big hug as always, and then took off with Toby to go swimming in the lake. He looked over at Candice, "Aren't you going to join them?"

She smiled at his grandfather, "In a minute."

"Jimmy says you're one of his best friends."

She smiled once more, "I am."

"So, you keep secrets for him?"

She giggled, "Of course, what are best friends for?"

She stopped and thought for a second, then

looked up at him standing there. "You know, I know."

"Of course, dear, I saw you last night."

"You saw me?" she whispered.

"We all did."

Her jaw dropped, "Please don't eat me."

He began laughing, "We don't do that, but we will need you to be quiet."

"I'll be quiet. I'll keep his secret and yours," she said.

"Thank you, Candice."

"He knows?" she asked him.

"Of course he knows, why do you think we came out here for his birthday, for his transition."

"He's known this whole time?" she asked him.

He chuckled, "Of course."

Reyna Young resides in California with her husband John Gillette and son, Logan. Together they run Last Doorway Productions, an independent film company. She is also known as TV Horror Hostess Miss Misery of Miss Misery's Movie Massacre. Author of the middle school grade Halloween Night Series and adult novels, Slasher Girl, and Welcome Home Natalie.

www.lastdoorwayproductions.com

Sneak Peek

Book 12

The Mummy Awakened on Mummy Street

1

Judy Michaels sauntered down the winding road on her way home from school. She felt a dread as she approached her house; her father was so fixated on renovating. Since he had taken a break from work, all he did was watch home renovation shows on TV and now he was obsessed with fixing up the basement. Judy knew the moment she got inside; her father would rope her into helping him and she had no interest in doing that.

"Judy, sweetheart, are you finally home?"

Her father shouted from the depths of the house.

Despite tiptoeing and trying to slip in unnoticed, she yelled back. "I'm afraid not, dad." She called back.

"Nice try, dear." Her father replied, as she heard his footsteps coming towards her.

"Come down here for a moment, won't you?"

Judy let out a deep sigh and dropped her backpack, running down the stairs.

"Fine, but only for a moment, I have so much homework to do."

She didn't have any homework to be honest, and all she wanted was to lounge on the couch and start her weekend off right. But duty called, as it always seems to do, when her father needed her help. It was never anything too pressing, only moving boxes around the house to make space. She knew this was coming as soon as she walked through the door. To her surprise, her father wasn't even packed yet. Her parents were leaving town for the weekend and her mother would surely be steamed if he wasn't ready to hit the road.

Judy helped her dad with a few boxes until her mother burst in the door, bubbling with excitement. Seeing her daughter placing boxes down, she knew her husband was up to his usual shenanigans.

Judy let out a heavy sigh. "May I watch some TV now, Mom?"

Her mother waved her along, "Of course."

Judy darted up the stairs to change into her coziest pajamas, eager to unwind. But the quietness was short-lived as the sound of a jackhammer roared from the basement, smashing and crashing and ruining any hope as to hearing the television.

She perched nervously on the creaky old couch, anxiously awaiting the departure of her parents.

The weekend stretched out before her like an endless abyss, but she had plans. Oh yes, she had plans. A little sleepover with her besties, approved by her dear auntie, who will be watching her for the weekend. Yet, the anticipation gnawed at her insides, twisting and turning like a writhing serpent. Where was her aunt? When would her parents finally take their leave? Suddenly, a guttural call from her father echoed through the house, beckoning her mother to the depths of the dank basement. But before she could even ponder the matter, a sharp ring of the doorbell pierced the air. Her heart pounding, Judy rushed to answer it, coming face to face with her friends, Natalie and

Kenny, brandishing sleeping bags and yummy snacks in tow. But something was off. It was very quiet. She called out to her parents, but the silence that met her was deafening. Fear prickled at her skin as she descended into the musty basement, on a mission to unravel what was going on. And what she saw there chilled her to the bone.

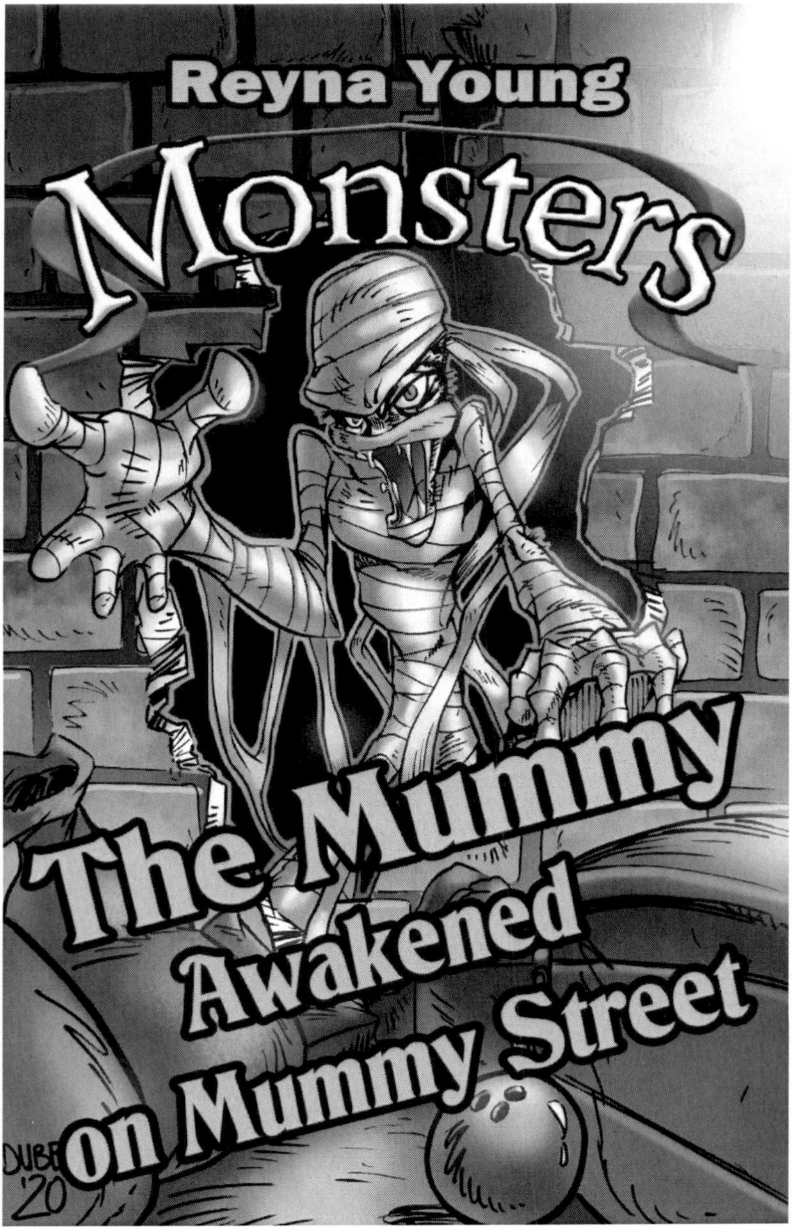
Reyna Young
Monsters
The Mummy
Awakened
on Mummy Street
DUBE
'20

Buy Book One Today!

www.lastdoorwayproductions.com

Read the scares - if you dare!

Monsters Unleashed

Monsters
Fan Mail

P.O. Box 225061
San Francisco, California
94122

Made in United States
North Haven, CT
07 August 2024

55810117R00067